A note to parents and teache

GU00730592

Welcome!

I wrote this book for a shared reading experience with children aged   ,
children are very curious about growing up, about the physical changes that come with that, and about adult life, including love and marriage. These are also years in which children are still willing to openly discuss these topics, and are very interested in having clear information and guidance from the adults who are important in their lives. I believe this chance should not be missed.

How to use this book:

- **Read with any age**—to help a child understand his or her past growth and future potential

- **Reflect on words of wisdom**—shared at the end of the story to deepen understanding

- **Become part of the story**—complete the self-portrait pages to guide more personal conversations

Why this book?

With my own children, I was able to find excellent books on the biological aspects of growing up, which have led to many conversations—both profound and humorous! But I did not find any resources that presented a more holistic picture of the process of physical, mental, emotional, and spiritual maturation and how all these elements can work together in the crafting of a life of personal fulfillment and service to others. This is the gap that I hope to fill with this book, in a way that is inspired by the Holy Writings of the Bahá'í Faith and by Bahá'í community life. I hope that this book may also speak to those from other spiritual traditions, and to those open to exploring new cultures and diverse beliefs.

In addition to representing my understanding of the maturation process, this book also draws on other powerfully constructive patterns of thinking and acting. Any sentence in the story could be used as a positive affirmation to help shape a child's day. The book also promotes mindfulness—expressed as self-reflection and prayer. Finally, I have tried to weave in the notion of a growth mindset, the ability to appreciate challenges and learn from them.

I hope you enjoy reading this book with the children you care about.
Catherine A. Honeyman

I am a baby.

I am loved and cared for.

I play, I laugh, and I cry.

I grow strong and healthy.

I make mistakes, and I learn from them.

Who do you love,
and who loves you?

I am a young child.

I have big feelings.

I learn to express myself.

I take care of my own body and my things.

I make mistakes, and I learn to pray about them.

How do you take care
of yourself and your things?

I am an older child.

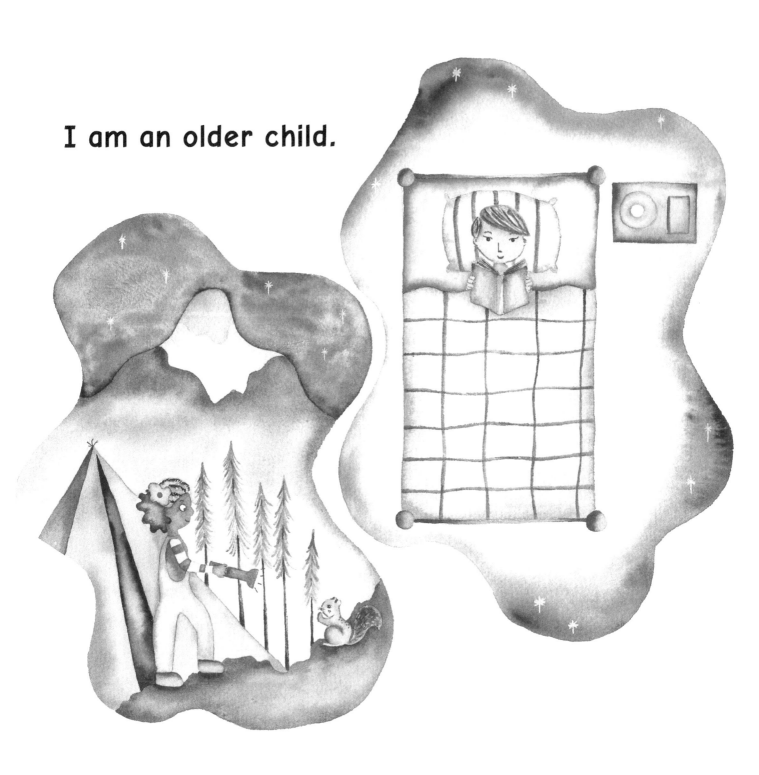

I start school, and I join a children's class.

I begin to master my feelings and develop my virtues.

I make friends, I listen to my friends, and I respect them.

I learn to read and write and to use numbers to unlock the doors of knowledge.

I am creative, I am thoughtful, I am unique, and I shine with a bright light.

I make mistakes, I pray about them, and I learn from them.

What do you love
to learn about?

I am a junior youth.

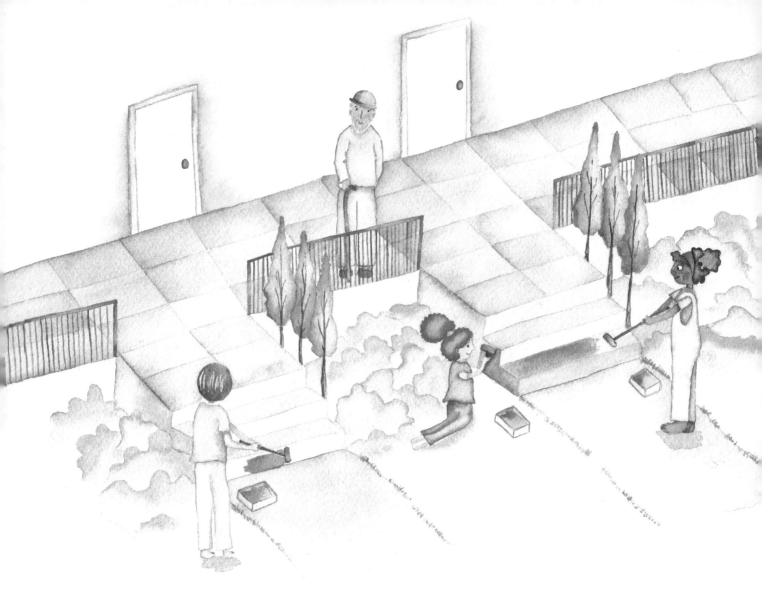

I advance in school, and I join a junior youth group.

I begin to analyze what is around me, in the light of science and faith.

I grow my virtues and I use them for service in my family and neighborhood.

I learn what qualities I like in other people, and what talents I have in myself.

My body begins to change, and I strive to feel healthy and happy and whole.

I discover what I love to do, and I do it better than anyone expects of me.

I become a good friend to others, and I resolve conflicts when I need to.

I make mistakes, and I learn to bring myself to account for them.

What do you know
about being a good friend?

I am a youth.

I do my best to keep learning, and I join a study circle to search for truth.

I discover and create, and I share my knowledge with others.

I take care of my body, my mind, my heart, and my spirit.

I start to see what work I could do, and I build my skills to prepare for it.

I seek freedom, but I respect my parents and the Holy Writings.

I desire independence, but I ask for advice when I need it.

I long for love, but I wait until I am ready for its responsibilities.

I make mistakes, I bring myself to account, I pray, and I learn more every day.

When would you be ready
for love and marriage?

I am an adult.

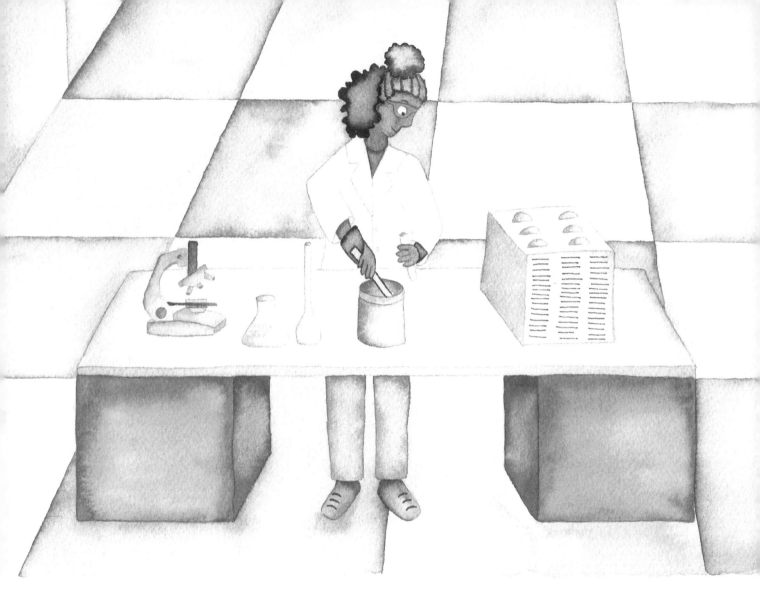

I work and I earn. I take care of my own needs and I give to help others.

If I wish to marry, I seek a friendship that can grow into lifelong love.

I search for someone who is truthful, generous, and kind.

Who will it be?

To make our choice, we serve our community together

and we learn about one another through joys and trials.

We lay the foundations of a fortress for wellbeing,

and we ask our parents if they consent to uniting our families in marriage.

In marriage, we learn new things about our hearts, our minds, and our bodies.

We face challenges we never expected,

and we overcome them with patience and consultation.

We seek guidance from others, from prayer, and from study of the Holy Writings.

Beyond love,

God gives me many other gifts.

I know my life is full of purpose, and I pursue it fully.

I make mistakes, I learn from them, and I continue to grow in life and love.

Wisdom from the Bahá'í Writings on Life and Love

Thoughts on how to live

"Be generous in prosperity, and thankful in adversity. Be worthy of the trust of thy neighbor, and look upon him with a bright and friendly face. Be a treasure to the poor, an admonisher to the rich, an answerer of the cry of the needy, a preserver of the sanctity of thy pledge. Be fair in thy judgment, and guarded in thy speech. Be unjust to no man, and show all meekness to all men. Be as a lamp unto them that walk in darkness, a joy to the sorrowful, a sea for the thirsty, a haven for the distressed, an upholder and defender of the victim of oppression. Let integrity and uprightness distinguish all thine acts. Be a home for the stranger, a balm to the suffering, a tower of strength for the fugitive. Be eyes to the blind, and a guiding light unto the feet of the erring. Be an ornament to the countenance of truth, a crown to the brow of fidelity, a pillar of the temple of righteousness, a breath of life to the body of mankind, an ensign of the hosts of justice, a luminary above the horizon of virtue, a dew to the soil of the human heart, an ark on the ocean of knowledge, a sun in the heaven of bounty, a gem on the diadem of wisdom, a shining light in the firmament of thy generation, a fruit upon the tree of humility." —Bahá'u'lláh

"O ye peoples of the world! Know assuredly that My commandments are the lamps of My loving providence among My servants, and the keys of My mercy for My creatures. . . .
     The Tongue of My power hath, from the heaven of My omnipotent glory, addressed to My creation these words: 'Observe My commandments, for the love of My beauty.'"
—Bahá'u'lláh

"O SON OF SPIRIT! I created thee rich, why dost thou bring thyself down to poverty? Noble I made thee, wherewith dost thou abase thyself? Out of the essence of knowledge I gave thee being, why seekest thou enlightenment from anyone beside Me? Out of the clay of love I molded thee, how dost thou busy thyself with another? Turn thy sight unto thyself, that thou mayest find Me standing within thee, mighty, powerful and self-subsisting."
—Bahá'u'lláh

Service to others

"Wherefore, O ye illumined youth, strive by night and by day to unravel the mysteries of the mind and spirit, and to grasp the secrets of the Day of God. Inform yourselves of the evidences that the Most Great Name hath dawned. Open your lips in praise. Adduce convincing arguments and proofs. Lead those who thirst to the fountain of life; grant ye true health to the ailing. Be ye apprentices of God; be ye physicians directed by God, and heal ye the sick among humankind. Bring those who have been excluded into the circle of intimate friends. Make the despairing to be filled with hope. Waken them that slumber; make the heedless mindful.

Such are the fruits of this earthly life. Such is the station of resplendent glory."
–'Abdu'l-Bahá

"You must manifest complete love and affection toward all mankind. Do not exalt yourselves above others, but consider all as your equals, recognizing them as the servants of one God. Know that God is compassionate toward all; therefore, love all from the depths of your hearts, prefer all religionists before yourselves, be filled with love for every race, and be kind toward the people of all nationalities. Never speak disparagingly of others, but praise without distinction. . . . Act in such a way that your heart may be free from hatred. Let not your heart be offended with anyone. If someone commits an error and wrong toward you, you must instantly forgive him. Do not complain of others. Refrain from reprimanding them, and if you wish to give admonition or advice, let it be offered in such a way that it will not burden the bearer. Turn all your thoughts toward bringing joy to hearts. Beware! Beware! lest ye offend any heart. Assist the world of humanity as much as possible. Be the source of consolation to every sad one, assist every weak one, be helpful to every indigent one, care for every sick one, be the cause of glorification to every lowly one, and shelter those who are overshadowed by fear.

In brief, let each one of you be as a lamp shining forth with the light of the virtues of the world of humanity. Be trustworthy, sincere, affectionate and replete with chastity. Be illumined, be spiritual, be divine, be glorious, be quickened of God, be a Bahá'í."
–'Abdu'l-Bahá

Purity and chastity

"Such a chaste and holy life, with its implications of modesty, purity, temperance, decency, and clean-mindedness, involves no less than the exercise of moderation in all that pertains to dress, language, amusements, and all artistic and literary avocations. It demands daily vigilance in the control of one's carnal desires and corrupt inclinations. It calls for the abandonment of a frivolous conduct, with its excessive attachment to trivial and often misdirected pleasures. It requires total abstinence from all alcoholic drinks, from opium, and from similar habit-forming drugs. . . . It can tolerate no compromise with the theories, the standards, the habits, and the excesses of a decadent age."
–Shoghi Effendi

"The Bahá'í youth should study the teachings on chastity and, with these in mind, should avoid any behavior which would arouse passions which would tempt them to violate them. In deciding what acts are permissible to them in the light of these considerations the youth must use their own judgement, following the guidance of their consciences and the advice of their parents.
If Bahá'í youth combine such personal purity with an attitude of uncensorious forbearance towards others they will find that those who may have criticized or even mocked them will come, in time, to respect them. They will, moreover, be laying a firm foundation for future married happiness." –The Universal House of Justice

"The proper use of the sex instinct is the natural right of every individual, and it is precisely for this very purpose that the institution of marriage has been established. The Bahá'ís do not believe in the suppression of the sex impulse but in its regulation and control."
–The Universal House of Justice

Marriage

"Bahá'í marriage is the commitment of the two parties one to the other, and their mutual attachment of mind and heart. Each must, however, exercise the utmost care to become thoroughly acquainted with the character of the other, that the binding covenant between them may be a tie that will endure forever. Their purpose must be this: to become loving companions and comrades and at one with each other for time and eternity. . . ." –'Abdu'l-Bahá

"Marriage is dependent upon the consent of both parties. Desiring to establish love, unity and harmony amidst Our servants, We have conditioned it, once the couple's wish is known, upon the permission of their parents. . . ." –Bahá'u'lláh

"And when He desired to manifest grace and beneficence to men, and to set the world in order, He revealed observances and created laws; among them He established the law of marriage, made it as a fortress for well-being and salvation, and enjoined it upon us in that which was sent down out of the heaven of sanctity in His Most Holy Book." –Bahá'u'lláh

Self-Portrait
and
Reflection Pages

* Note: The prayers included on the following pages are from the writings of 'Abdu'l-Bahá, the son of Bahá'u'lláh.

All About Me as a Baby

O Thou peerless Lord! Let this suckling babe be nursed from the breast of Thy loving-kindness, guard it within the cradle of Thy safety and protection and grant that it be reared in the arms of Thy tender affection.*

(photo or drawing)

People who love me: _____

_____

My first words: _____

_____

What I love to do: _____

_____

_____

_____

All About Me as a Young Child

[photo or drawing]

(photo or drawing)

My first sentences: _____

_____

What I try to do by myself: _____

_____

My favorite prayer: _____

_____

_____

*O Lord! I am a child;
enable me to grow
beneath the shadow
of Thy loving-kindness.
I am a tender plant;
cause me to be
nurtured through
the outpourings
of the clouds
of Thy bounty.
I am a sapling
of the garden of love;
make me into
a fruitful tree.*

*Thou art the Mighty
and the Powerful,
and Thou art the
All-Loving,
the All-Knowing,
the All-Seeing.**

All About Me as an Older Child

(photo or drawing)

O my Lord! O my Lord! . . .
Deliver me from darkness,
make me a brilliant light;
free me from unhappiness,
make me flower of the
rose-garden; suffer me
to become a servant
of Thy threshold
and confer upon me
the disposition and nature
of the righteous; make me
a cause of bounty
to the human world
and crown my head
with the diadem
of eternal life.*

Virtues I am developing: _____
_____

My first friends and what I like about them: _____
_____
_____

What I love to learn about: _____
_____
_____

All About Me as a Junior Youth

(photo or drawing)

Praise and glory be to Thee, O Lord my God! This is a choice sapling which Thou hast planted in the meads of Thy love and hast nurtured with the fingers of Thy Lordship. Thou hast watered it from the well-spring of everlasting life which streameth forth from the gardens of Thy oneness and Thou hast caused the clouds of Thy tender mercy to shower Thy favors upon it. It hath now grown and developed beneath the shelter of Thy blessings which are manifest from the Dayspring of Thy divine essence.*

My first efforts to serve my community: _____

_____

Some of my special talents: _____

_____

What I know about being a good friend: _____

_____

What I know about resolving conflict: _____

_____

All About Me as a Youth

O Lord! Make this youth radiant and confer Thy bounty upon this poor creature. Bestow upon him knowledge, grant him added strength at the break of every morn and guard him within the shelter of Thy protection so that he may be freed from error, may devote himself to the service of Thy Cause, may guide the wayward, lead the hapless, free the captives and awaken the heedless, that all may be blessed with Thy remembrance and praise.
Thou art the Mighty and the Powerful.*

(photo or drawing)

How I keep my body, mind, and spirit healthy: _____

_____

How I am preparing for adult life and work: _____

_____

Trusted people who give me good advice: _____

_____

Why I will wait to be ready for love and marriage: _____

_____

All About Me as an Adult

(photo or drawing)

O Lord, help Thou Thy loved ones to acquire knowledge and the sciences and arts, and to unravel the secrets that are treasured up in the inmost reality of all created beings. Make them to hear the hidden truths that are written and embedded in the heart of all that is. Make them to be ensigns of guidance amongst all creatures, and piercing rays of the mind shedding forth their light in this, the "first life." Make them to be leaders unto Thee, guides unto Thy path, runners urging men on to Thy Kingdom. Thou verily art the Powerful, the Protector, the Potent, the Defender, the Mighty, the Most Generous.*

My goals for work and service to others: _____

_____

Qualities I seek in my life partner: _____

_____

Gifts God has given me: _____

_____

My purpose and goals in life: _____

_____

_____

Some Ideas for Growing Up Learning Goals

Self
- Use please, thank you, excuse me, and I'm sorry
- Know how to express what you need and want
- Regulate your own emotions
- Learn to listen and resolve conflict
- Clean and dress yourself, do laundry
- Know how to sew, to repair and care for your clothes
- Clean your bed, room, desk
- Entertain yourself without TV
- Swim, bicycle, jog/run
- Find a physical activity you love
- Repair an electrical device
- Fix a bicycle or car
- Build and tend a fire

Family & Others
- Care for plants, grow food
- Plan and prepare a meal and dessert
- Clean the house: sweep, mop, vacuum, sanitize, wash dishes
- Care for an animal
- Care for a child
- Help to fight against prejudice, promote justice
- Contribute to community life and help those in need
- Reduce, reuse, recycle, and fight climate change

Spirit & Arts
- Create beauty around you
- Play an instrument, learn a fine art
- Investigate the truth for yourself
- Know the history of religions
- Know and follow the principles and laws of your Faith
- Learn by heart poems, proverbs, prayers, and Holy Writings
- Attend community gatherings and contribute to them

Studies
- Letters, numbers, reading and writing
- Arithmetic, algebra, geometry, calculus, statistics
- Type on a computer, learn to code and program
- Search for accurate information on the internet
- Speak at least two languages
- Express your ideas in writing and in front of groups
- Read and analyze the news
- Investigate topics that interest you
- Experiment to answer a scientific question
- Know how your family history and world history connect
- Read books and articles written by people you admire

Work
- Know your special talents
- Know your interests
- Find a vocation / career goal
- Know what to study and what skills to practice, to prepare for your vocation
- Complete a job on time and to good quality
- Identify, market, and deliver a needed product or service
- Budget and save
- Talk to adults to understand their careers

My Growing Up Learning Goals

Choose some goals that matter to you and write them below.
Use the next page to add more goals.

Goal	What level are your skills now? Mark when you advance.			
	Beginner	Skilled	Advanced	Expert
1.				
2.				
3.				
4.				
5.				
6.				
7.				
8.				
9.				
10.				

My Growing Up Learning Goals

Choose some goals that matter to you and write them below.

Goal	What level are your skills now? Mark when you advance.			
	Beginner	Skilled	Advanced	Expert
11.				
12.				
13.				
14.				
15.				
16.				
17.				
18.				
19.				
20.				

Lightning Source UK Ltd.
Milton Keynes UK
UKHW021058170922
409001UK00002B/48